To my mom, for putting up with our sibling shenanigans, and for always encouraging my imagination —PS

For Will, Dylan, Jacob, Tom, and Eddy, from Uncle Joe —JB

DIAL
BOOKS FOR YOUNG READERS
A division of Penguin Young Readers Group
Published by The Penguin Group • Penguin Group (USA) Inc., 375 Hudson Street, New York, NY 10014, U.S.A. • Penguin Group (Canada), 90 Eglinton Avenue East, Suite 700, Toronto, Ontario, Canada M4P 2Y3 (a division of Pearson Penguin Canada Inc.) • Penguin Books Ltd, 80 Strand, London WC2R 0RL, England • Penguin Ireland, 25 St. Stephen's Green, Dublin 2, Ireland (a division of Penguin Books Ltd) • Penguin Group (Australia), 250 Camberwell Road, Camberwell, Victoria 3124, Australia (a division of Pearson Australia Group Pty Ltd) • Penguin Books India Pvt Ltd, 11 Community Centre, Panchsheel Park, New Delhi - 110 017, India • Penguin Group (NZ), 67 Apollo Drive, Rosedale, North Shore 0632, New Zealand (a division of Pearson New Zealand Ltd) • Penguin Books (South Africa) (Pty) Ltd, 24 Sturdee Avenue, Rosebank, Johannesburg 2196, South Africa • Penguin Books Ltd, Registered Offices: 80 Strand, London WC2R 0RL, England

Designed by Lily Malcom
Text set in Rockwell
Manufactured in China on acid-free paper
10 9 8 7 6 5 4 3 2

To Jessica Garrison and James Proimos, with special thanks and a grateful heart —PS

Library of Congress Cataloging-in-Publication Data

Smallcomb, Pam, date.
Earth to Clunk / by Pam Smallcomb ; pictures by Joe Berger.
  p. cm.
Summary: For a school assignment, a boy reluctantly writes a letter to Clunk of the planet Quazar, sending his older sister with it, but as more letters and packages are exchanged, he realizes that having an alien pen pal can be fun.
ISBN 978-0-8037-3439-5 (hardcover)
[1. Pen pals—Fiction. 2. Extraterrestrial beings—Fiction. 3. Brothers and sisters—Fiction.] I. Berger, Joe, date, ill. II. Title.
PZ7.S63914Ear 2011
[E]—dc22
                                    2010020621

The artwork was created using pencil, pen, and ink, and colored using Adobe Photoshop.

EARTH TO CLUNK

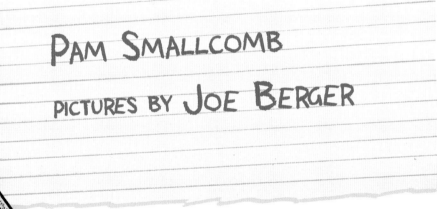

Pam Smallcomb

Pictures By Joe Berger

Dial Books for Young Readers
an imprint of Penguin Group (USA) Inc.

Today Mr. Zookian said I have to write to my pen pal.
His name is Clunk.

"He lives on the planet Quazar," said Mr. Zookian.
"Write him a letter and send him something from Earth."

I don't want a pen pal named
Clunk from the planet Quazar.
I'm not writing a letter.

I'm sending Clunk my big sister.

THAT will teach him to have a pen pal from Earth.

I got a package from Clunk today.

He sent me
a Zoid.

I don't like Clunk or his stupid Zoid.

It follows me everywhere.

I'm sending Clunk all my dirty socks.

THAT will teach him to have a pen pal from Earth.

I got another package from Clunk today.
He sent me these three Forps.

I don't like Clunk, or his stupid Zoid
(it's STILL following me around), or
these three Forps.

Forps smell like dog food.

I'm sending Clunk a picture I drew of Earth.

It is so scary, he will never want
a pen pal from Earth again.

Clunk sent me a drawing of Quazar.
Even my hair was scared when I saw it.

If it weren't for Zoid, I wouldn't have slept at all.

I'm sending Clunk an electric toothbrush, a toilet plunger, and a string of Christmas lights.

He will be so confused, he'll never send me another thing.

I got a package from Clunk today.

I don't know what these things are,
but I'm going to put them inside the closet and lock it.

Bad news.

Mom found out about my big sister.
"You tell Clunk to send her right
back. She has chores to do."

I write Clunk a note:

MY MOM WANTS MY SISTER BACK.

I DO NOT.

YOU DECIDE

I put the note under some old lasagna I found in the fridge. It is so gross, I am sure Clunk will never send another package to Earth again.

I wait . . .
and wait . . .
and wait . . .

No package.

Nope.
Nada.
Zip.

Maybe the lasagna was too gross.

Maybe my big sister is bossing him around
and he has no time for his pen pal on Earth.

Maybe Clunk will never send me another
package, ever.

I think I miss getting packages from Clunk.

I got a package from Clunk today!
Inside is a disgusting glob of something.
And my big sister.

"You are so dead,"
she says to me.
But then Mom gives
her chores to do.

I look at the glob in the box.
There is a note underneath.

It says:

I LIKED THE GLOB YOU SENT TO EAT. I DID NOT LIKE YOUR SISTER. HERE IS A GLOB FROM QUAZAR.

The glob from Quazar tastes like ice cream, only chewy.

I ask Mom,
"Can Clunk come
for a sleepover?"

"If you clean the
basement first,"
she says.

I put some
baseball
cards in a
package for
Clunk.
I write a note
and ask him
to come for a
sleepover.
Anyone who
doesn't like
my big sister
is okay by me.

I wait.

And wait.

And wait.

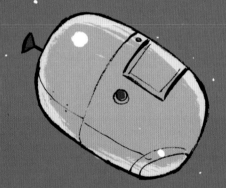

Finally . . .

Clunk is HERE!

Clunk and I are building a fort in the basement.
It has to be strong to keep out my big sister.
Zoid will help.

But Clunk
says it will
take more
than Zoid to
keep her out.

KEEP OUT!

He says we're going to need the stuff I locked in the closet . . .